To my really really brave friend Paul d'Auria
K. G.

For Jon
N. S.

A BODLEY HEAD BOOK : 0 370 32733 0

Published in Great Britain in 2002 by The Bodley Head,
an imprint of Random House Children's Books

1 3 5 7 9 10 8 6 4 2

Text copyright © Kes Gray 2002
Illustrations copyright © Nick Sharratt 2002

Papers used by Random House Children's Books are natural, recyclable products made from wood grown in sustainable forests.
The manufacturing processes conform to the environmental regulations of the country of origin.

RANDOM HOUSE CHILDREN'S BOOKS
61-63 Uxbridge Rd, London W5 5SA
A division of The Random House Group Ltd.

RANDOM HOUSE AUSTRALIA (PTY) LTD
20 Alfred Street, Milsons Point, Sydney,
New South Wales 2061, Australia

RANDOM HOUSE NEW ZEALAND LTD
18 Poland Road, Glenfield, Auckland 10, New Zealand

RANDOM HOUSE (PTY) LTD
Endulini, 5A Jubilee Road, Parktown 2193, South Africa

THE RANDOM HOUSE GROUP Limited Reg. No. 954009
www.randomhouse.co.uk

A CIP catalogue record for this book is available from the British Library.

Printed and bound in Singapore by Tien Wah Press (Pty) Ltd

Really, Really

Kes Gray & Nick Sharratt

THE BODLEY HEAD
LONDON

Daisy was very excited.

She'd never had a babysitter before.

Daisy's *mum* was very late.

"Daisy meet Angela, Angela meet Daisy!" said Daisy's *mum*,

kissing Daisy on the forehead and then running down

the path to the taxi waiting outside.

Angela the babysitter closed the front door and smiled at Daisy. "Why are you eating paper?" she asked.

"I'm not eating paper," said Daisy.

"Really?" said Angela.

"Really, really," fibbed Daisy.

"You must be hungry," said Angela.
"What do you usually have
for tea?"
"Ice-cream and chips," said Daisy.
"Really?" said Angela.
"Really, really," fibbed Daisy.

"Have you ever had a babysitter before?" asked Angela.

"Hundreds!" said Daisy.

"Really?" said Angela.

"Really, really," fibbed Daisy.

"Would you like a glass of milk?" asked Angela.

"I'm only allowed lemonade," said Daisy.

"Really?" said Angela.

"Really, really," fibbed Daisy.

"What time do you usually go to bed?" asked Angela.
"Midnight at the earliest," said Daisy.
"Really?" said Angela.
"Really, really," fibbed Daisy.

"Do you need to have a bath?" asked Angela.

"I don't get dirty," said Daisy.

"Really?" said Angela.

"Really, really," fibbed Daisy.

"What time do you put your pyjamas on?" asked Angela.

"I always sleep in my clothes," said Daisy.

"Really?" said Angela.

"Really, really," fibbed Daisy.

"Shall we sit down and do some reading?" asked Angela.

"My mum prefers it if I play games," said Daisy.

"What sort of games?" asked Angela.

"Bouncing on the settee and sliding on the table," said Daisy, "until ten o'clock."

"Really?" said Angela.

"Really, really," fibbed Daisy.

"Then we watch videos till midnight," said Daisy.

"Really?" said Angela.

"Really, really," fibbed Daisy.

At midnight Daisy heard a taxi pull up outside her house. "I'm feeling very sleepy all of a sudden," said Daisy, jumping off the sofa and scooting upstairs to bed.

Angela opened the front door and Daisy's *mum* tiptoed in.

"Hello Angela," whispered Daisy's *mum*. "Has Daisy been a good girl? She did give *you my* note didn't she? She did have a proper tea didn't she? She did have a bath and wash her hair? She did put clean pyjamas on didn't she? She was in bed by eight wasn't she? And she didn't charge around the house like a mad thing did she?"

Angela put her hands behind her back and crossed her fingers.

"She's been as good as gold," said Angela. "She's been a little angel."

"Really?" asked Daisy's *mum.*

Great meets

Amongst the many different grand prix meetings are some extremely famous annual events, including the Golden Gala in Rome and, since 1961, the Golden Spike in Ostrava in the Czech Republic. The Bislett Games in Oslo, first held in 1924, are among the most famous. Over 50 world records have been broken on the famous red track of Bislett's stadium.

The Weltklasse

One of the very first major grand prix meetings was held in the Swiss city of Zurich in 1928. Since that time, the annual Weltklasse meeting has attracted many of the world's best athletes. The 26,000 sell-out crowds at the Letzigrund stadium have seen 25 new world records set, such as Yelena Isinbayeva's 2009 record-breaking pole vault.

GREAT SPORTING STATS

The IAAF divide meetings into grand prix and, above them, super grand prix. In 2009, there were 13 grand prix, starting with Melbourne in Australia in March, and ending with Rieti in Italy in September. The five super grand prix in 2009 were: Qatar, Athletissima (Switzerland), London Grand Prix, Herculis (Monaco) and DN Galan (Stockholm, Sweden).

Russian pole vaulter Yelena Isinbayeva celebrates setting a new world record of 5.06m at the 2009 Weltklasse meeting in Zurich.

Gold and Diamond Leagues

For over a **decade** some of the greatest IAAF athletics meetings were grouped together to form a Golden League, with top prize money for the best athletes. For the 2010 season, after some epic performances and events, the competition was revamped into the IAAF Diamond League.

Share of the spoils

Starting in 1998 with six key athletics meetings each year, the Golden League offered top athletes the chance to win a share of a US$1 million (£675,000) jackpot if they remained unbeaten.

In 2009, for example, the prize was shared by Russian pole vaulter Yelena Isinbayeva, Ethiopian long-distance runner Kenenisa Bekele and US sprinter Sanya Richards.

Yelena Isinbayeva, Kenenisa Bekele and Sanya Richards pose with gold bars – part of the US$1 million jackpot they shared for winning all of their Golden League events.

Major meetings

The Golden League meetings were held solely in famous European athletics **stadia**, including the Stade de France in Paris and Rome's Olympic Stadium. A total of 31 world records were set in the Golden League. Only one year, 2002, did not see a world record set in a Golden League meeting.

Going for gold

Only three athletes have won the Golden League jackpot prize outright for remaining unbeaten in their event: 800m runner Maria Mutola from Mozambique in 2003, Russian triple jumper Tatyana Lebedeva in 2005 and Kenyan 800m runner Pamela Jelimo in 2008. Jelimo was only 19 years old when in 2008, she won her sixth Golden League 800m race in Brussels.

Maria Mutola celebrates her 800m win at the Golden League meeting in Brussels, Belgium, 2003.

GREAT SPORTING STATS

US sprinter Allyson Felix had a brilliant 2010 season, winning 21 out of the 22 races she entered. Overall, she outperformed her rivals in both the 200m and 400m races to be the only athlete to win two Diamond League events in the same season. Felix's one defeat came in the New York Diamond League meeting.

IAAF Diamond League

The Diamond League began in 2010. It features an expanded series of 14 meetings, starting in Qatar in the Middle East in May and ending with two finals meetings in Zurich and Brussels in August. The leading athlete in each of the 32 different athletics events at the end of the year wins a diamond trophy. The total prize money on offer in the 2010 Diamond League season was US$6.63 million (around £4.2 million).

City marathons

Marathons are the ultimate tests of long-distance competitive running. They are gruelling, lung-busting races held over 42.195 kilometres (26.2 miles). Leading marathon competitions are held in the world's major cities, where they attract huge crowds.

UK long-distance runner Paula Radcliffe crosses the line to win the 2007 New York City Marathon. Radcliffe has won eight major city marathons.

Charity runners

Elite marathon runners are often paid to take part in the best city marathons, and race ahead of thousands of **amateur** athletes. Many amateurs are club runners or enter for the fitness challenge. Others take part, sometimes in funny costumes, in order to raise money for charity. In 2006, the former British Olympic rower Sir Steve Redgrave raised £1.8 million to help combat childhood leukaemia by completing the London Marathon.

New York City Marathon

Held in November since 1970, the New York City Marathon is one of the greatest city marathons. In 2009, 43,741 competitors started the race, with Meb Keflezighi becoming the first male US winner in New York since 1982.

London Marathon

The London Marathon is usually held in April. The event, which began in 1981, attracts high-class athletes who race along a course winding around the River Thames through central London. Germany's Irina Mikitenko was victorious in the women's event in both 2008 and 2009. The current women's world record was set by British athlete Paula Radcliffe in London in 2003.

World Marathon Majors

Since 2006 five of the world's leading city marathons – London, Chicago, Boston, Berlin and New York – have formed part of a Majors competition. The leading five finishers in each of these marathons win points. The man and woman who scores the most points over a two-year period wins US$500,000 (£338,000).

GREAT SPORTING STATS

Both the men's and women's world marathon records were set in city marathons. Ethiopian runner Haile Gebreselassie managed 2 hours, 3 minutes, 59 seconds in 2008 in Berlin, and Paula Radcliffe broke the women's world record in Chicago in 2002. She set the current world record of 2 hours 15 minutes, 25 seconds at the London Marathon the following year.

Runners in the London Marathon pass famous landmarks, such as Tower Bridge, on their way to the finish line.

The Asian Games

Each continent holds its own major athletics event, either as a pure athletics competition, or as part of a multi-sports event. Held since 1951, the four-yearly Asian Games feature competitions for a number of sports, including baseball, swimming and martial arts, such as judo and taekwondo. Athletics, however, is a hugely popular part of the competition.

The Khalifa Stadium in Doha, Qatar is lit up by fireworks during the opening ceremony for the 2006 Asian Games.

Bidding cities

Asian cities, backed by their countries' governments, bid for the right to **host** the Asian Games. In 2000, for example, a vote saw Doha in Qatar beat Kuala Lumpur (in Malaysia), Hong Kong and Delhi (in India) to host the 2006 games. The 2010 Asian Games were held in the Chinese city of Guangzhou. Over 40 Asian countries took part.

Traditional dominance

Three nations – China, South Korea and Japan – usually dominate the final medal table, but many other nations have enjoyed notable successes at the Asian Games. For example, the Indian women's 4x400m **relay** team has won gold at the past two Asian Games. Kazakhstan has also traditionally been strong in power field events, such as the discus and shot put.

Drama at Doha

The 2006 Asian Games in Doha was the first time the Asian Games was held in the Middle East. There was plenty of drama in athletics, with ten new Games records set. Bahrain's six gold medals (all in middle- or long-distance running, as well as the women's 200m) saw it come second in the medal table behind a powerful Chinese team. The margin of victory in one event was extraordinary – Zhang Wenxiu of China won the women's hammer by a massive margin of 9.02 metres.

GREAT SPORTING STATS

The 2006 Asian Games athletics medal table

Country	Medals		
	G	S	B
China	14	9	8
Bahrain	6	5	3
Japan	5	9	13
Saudi Arabia	5	0	2
Kazakhstan	4	4	1

China's Zhang Wenxiu throws the hammer en route to victory at the Asian Games.

European Championships

The European Championships was first held in 1934 and has been held every four years ever since. It attracts top athletes from across Europe, competing in some of the most famous athletics stadia in the world.

Top class competition

With over 1,400 athletes competing from 50 European nations, including athletics powerhouses such as Germany, Russia, France and Spain, the competition is often intense. This is especially the case in field athletics, where Eastern European nations have been strong for many decades. The world record for the men's hammer throw, for example, was set at the European Championships in 1986 by Yuriy Sedykh from the **Soviet Union** and has not been bettered since. Sedykh's record is one of 34 world records set at the European Championships over the years.

Heike Drechsler wins the long jump at the 1990 European Championships. Drechsler was from the former East Germany, one of the most dominant field athletics nations.

Portugal's Francis Obikwelu (far left) powers to the line to win the 200m at the 2006 European Championships.

GREAT SPORTING STATS

The Soviet Union, with 121 golds, leads the European Championships all-time medals table. In recent years, the competition has been more open. At the 2010 European Championships, 16 countries won the 47 gold medals available to athletes. A total of 25 nations won a medal.

Packed stadia

Thirteen different countries have hosted the European Championships. After the 2010 competition in Barcelona, Spain, the event will be held once every two years. The 2012 competition will be held for the third time in Finland's historic Olympiastadion, the site of the 1952 Olympic Games.

Championship winner

Athletes are awarded gold, silver and bronze medals for finishing in the top three places in each event. In 2006, there was no bronze medal awarded in the 100m women's hurdles because Germany's Kirsten Bolm and Ireland's Derval O'Rourke both finished the race in 12.72 seconds, and were each awarded silver medals.

The Pan American Games

Held once every four years, the Pan American Games is a multi-sport event. Its events are open to athletes from countries in North and South America and the island nations of the Caribbean.

Early games

After plans to hold an event were interrupted by World War II (1939–1945), the first Pan American Games began in Argentina in 1951. Early competitions were held in Mexico, the USA, Brazil and Canada. The 1971 games in Cali, Colombia, were notable for a world record in the triple jump and Jamaica's Don Quarrie running the 200m in 19.86 seconds – a games record that still stands some 40 years later.

Don Quarrie from Jamaica wins a 200m race. Quarrie won both the 100m and 200m at the 1971 Pan American Games.

Nations large and small

All 42 countries in the region now send athletes to the Pan American Games. These include giants such as the USA, with a population of over 300 million, and Brazil with over 190 million. At the other end of the scale is Antigua and Barbuda whose small population of just about 90,000 people celebrated when Brendan Christian won the men's 200m sprint at the 2007 games.

Rio 2007

The 2007 games were held in Rio de Janeiro in Brazil and saw some very close competition. In the women's discus, for example, just one centimetre separated first and second place with Cuba's Yarelis Barrios triumphant. A number of new championship records were set at these games, including the women's 10,000m, pole vault and triple jump.

Athletes in the 4x400m relay exchange **batons** on a rain-soaked track at the 2007 Pan American Games. The event was won by the Bahamas, half a second ahead of the US team.

GREAT SPORTING STATS

Of the 47 different athletics competitions held at the Pan American Games, the following countries hold the most championship records.

Country	Records
Cuba	18
USA	12
Brazil	5
Jamaica	5
Canada	5

American dominance

The USA leads the all-time medal table in athletics at the Games. In recent years, however, the USA has sometimes sent its younger or reserve athletes, rather than its superstars who were training for other competitions. This may explain why the men's discus and the women's shot put records, both set in 1983, have yet to be broken.

World Indoor Championships

Indoor events tend to take place in the northern hemisphere, where large arenas and indoor tracks allow top athletes to compete in the winter season. In 1985, an exciting new biannual competition was founded by the IAAF – the World Indoor Championships.

Spain's Natalia Rodriguez leads the women's 1,500m race at the 2010 World Indoor Championships.

Differing events

Because of limited space, not all athletics events are held at a World Indoor Championships. Of the four throws, only the shot put appears, whilst the longest race on the track is usually the 3,000m. Race walkers, who normally compete outdoors over 10,000m, 20,000m and 50,000m distances, race only 3,000m indoors.

Track facts

All World Indoor Championships feature a 200m track that has steeply-banked bends to aid fast running. The track is usually only four lanes wide, which means tight, cramped racing at times. The 100m sprints are reduced to 60m in length on a straight piece of track, usually running down the centre of the arena.

Indoor heptathlon

Indoors, male decathletes take part in a seven-event heptathlon competing in the 60m sprint, long jump, shot put, high jump, 60m hurdles, pole vault, and five laps of the track in a 1,000m race. At the 2008 World Indoor Championships, US decathlete Brian Clay won the heptathlon to add to his Olympic decathlon win the same year.

Indoor venues

The Championships are always held in March in countries as varied as Japan, Canada, Germany and, in 2012, Turkey. In 2010, the event was held at the Aspire Dome in Qatar. This brand new facility seats 15,000 spectators.

GREAT SPORTING STATS

There have been some outstanding repeat performances at the World Indoor Championships, but two female runners stand out in particular:

Maria Mutola — 800m runner from Mozambique
Medals: 7 gold, 1 silver, 1 bronze.

Natalya Nazarova — 400m and 4x400m relay runner from Russia
Medals: 7 gold, 2 silver.

Brian Clay throws the shot put at the 2008 World Indoor Championships heptathlon competition.

The World Championships

When athletes lobbied for their own dedicated world championship, away from the Olympics, the IAAF founded the World Championships in Athletics in 1983. The event has since grown in popularity. The 2009 event in Berlin was watched by over 500,000 live spectators.

Biannual event

The World Championships were originally held once every four years, but since 1991 they have been held every two years, though never in an Olympic year. They are held in August or early September and offer ten days of exciting athletics action.

Ed Moses of the USA (right) wins the 400m hurdles at the 1987 World Championships. Moses won an astonishing 122 consecutive races between 1977 and 1987.

Osaka action

The 2007 Championships were held in the Japanese city of Osaka. Over 1,970 athletes, from 200 nations, took part in 47 medal-winning events, 23 for women and 24 for men, with the 50km race walk being the extra male event. Standout performances included those of the US relay teams, which won all four relay events, and Germany's Franka Dietzsch winning her third World Championship in the discus throw at the age of 39.

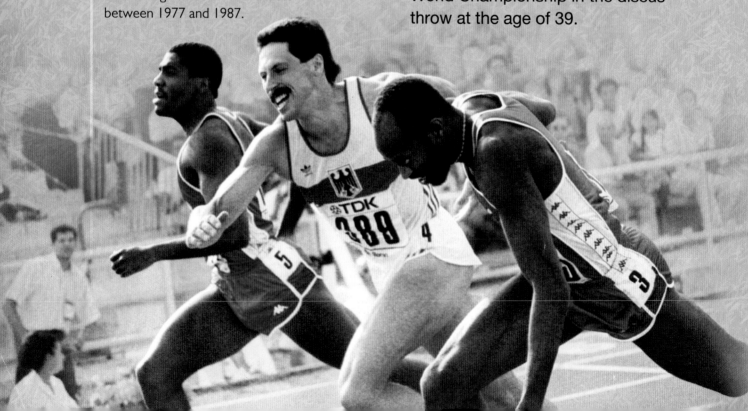

Brilliant Berlin

The 2009 World Championships in Berlin didn't disappoint, either. There were many notable performances, including Ethiopia's Kenenisa Bekele becoming the first man to win both the 5,000m and 10,000m at the same World Championships. An amazing 241 athletes recorded **personal bests** in their event, none more memorable than Jamaica's Usain Bolt who broke both his 100m and 200m world records with scintillating runs.

World Championship hosts

The World Championships have been held in Canada, but never the USA, whilst Finland, Japan and Germany are the three countries to have hosted the event twice. In 2011, the World Championships returns to Asia in Daegu, South Korea, with the 2013 event to be held in the Luzhniki Stadium in the Russian capital, Moscow.

GREAT SPORTING STATS

Leading medal winning nations at the World Championships

Country	G	S	B
USA	120	66	64
Russia	37	52	43
Kenya	31	27	25
Germany	28	23	36
Soviet Union	22	25	28

(Soviet Union up to 1991, Russia from 1993 onwards.)

Poland's Anita Włodarczyk competes in the women's hammer throw at the 2009 World Championships in Berlin. She won the event and broke the world record with a throw of 77.96m.

The Olympics

The world's biggest sporting event is held once every four years for 17 days in late summer. The Summer Olympic Games attracts over 10,000 competitors, competing in more than 30 sports. Athletics events are some of the most popular and exciting to watch.

Going for gold

For most track and field athletes, the Olympics is the peak of their competitive careers. Getting to the Olympics is the goal of many, but only the very best get the chance to win a highly-prized Olympic gold, silver or bronze medal.

In 2008, Olympic medals went to Christine Ohuruogu (centre, gold), Shericka Williams (left, silver) and Sanya Richards (right, bronze) in the women's 400m.

Olympic hosts

Hosting the Summer Olympics is a great honour. Different world cities bid and the International Olympic Committee (IOC) decides who will host an Olympics many years in advance. The hosting country has a mammoth task ahead. World-class sports facilities have to be built, as well as a giant **Olympic village** to house and feed over 10,000 athletes and thousands more sports coaches and officials. These facilities will then be enjoyed by future generations.

The Olympic Stadium in Sydney, Australia hosted the 2000 Games. It held a record-breaking 110,000 spectators.

The Greek team enter the stadium at the opening ceremony of the 2008 Olympics.

Olympic traditions

The modern Olympic Games began in 1896 as a revival of the Ancient Greek games held at Olympia as far back as 776BCE. Various traditions accompany the modern Olympics, from the burning of the Olympic flame throughout the event, to the elaborate opening and closing ceremonies.

Great Olympians

Every Olympic Games witnesses some outstanding performances from top athletes. At the 2008 Games, for example, there were five world records and 17 Olympic records set. Here are some of the truly great Olympic athletes.

Merlene Ottey (left) appeared at an incredible seven Olympics, winning three silver and five bronze medals. Here she is pipped to the finishing line by Gail Devers in the 1996 Olympics women's 100m final.

Female pioneers

Women were not allowed to compete in Olympic athletics until 1928 and then only in a small number of events. Dutch athlete Fanny Blankers-Koen shattered old-fashioned views of how delicate women were with a stunning four gold medals at the 1948 games in the 100m, 200m, 80m hurdles and the 4x100m relay. Sixty years later, Russian Gulnara Samitova-Galkina won the first ever women's Olympic 3,000m steeplechase final, becoming the first woman to finish in under 9 minutes.

The flying Finns

In the 1920s, the legendary 'Flying Finn', Paavo Nurmi, was almost unstoppable. He won three silver and an incredible nine gold medals at three Olympics (1920, 1924 and 1928). Fifty years later, another Finnish athlete, Lasse Virén, would win the 5,000m and 10,000m races at both the 1972 and 1976 Olympics.

GREAT SPORTING STATS

US athlete Carl Lewis has one of the best Olympic records of all time. In four Olympics he won nine gold medals and one silver medal:

Long jump 1984, 1988, 1992, 1996
100m 1984, 1988
200m 1984, 1992 (silver)
4x100m 1984, 1992

Track and field stars

On the track, US sprinters have often shone, including Jesse Owens, Michael Johnson and Carl Lewis. In field events, US athlete Al Oerter famously won the discus at four Olympics in a row, whilst Russian pole vaulter Yelena Isinbayeva (see p.7) won back-to-back golds at the 2004 and 2008 Olympics. Tamara Press of the Soviet Union also won gold medals in both the shot put and the discus.

Lightning bolt

At the 2008 Olympics, all eyes were on a young Jamaican sprinter who had got the athletics world very excited. Usain Bolt didn't disappoint, beating the opposition in the 100m, 200m and 4x100m relay, winning gold medals and setting astonishing new world records in all three events.

Usain Bolt celebrates as he blasts his way to winning the 2008 Olympics men's 200m sprint in a world record time of 19.30 seconds.

The Paralympics

The Parallel Olympics (or **Paralympics**) are a competition for elite athletes with disabilities. They are now held at the same venues as the Olympics shortly after a Summer Olympics has finished, and attract increasingly large crowds and followers on television.

Great growth

The first full Paralympics was held in Rome in 1960, with around 400 competitors taking part. Since then, the competition has blossomed. At the 2008 Paralympics in Beijing, for example, there were 1,035 competitors taking part in athletics, representing over 120 countries.

Classification

Paralympic athletes are sportspeople with a physical disability or visual **impairment**. They compete with others of a similar disability level by being grouped into classes. This is called classification (see p.27).

One of the standout athletes of the 2008 Paralympics was Oscar Pistorius (left). The South African won gold in the 100m, 200m and 400m in the T44 category for **amputees**.

Top Paralympians
complete the marathon in
under 1 hour 45 minutes.

**GREAT SPORTING
STATS**

Paralympic adaptions

Many Paralympic athletics events
are run in the same way as events
in the Olympics. Wheelchair-bound
athletes may sit in their chair as they
perform a throw in a field event. On
the track, racing in specially-designed
wheelchairs is fast, furious and ranges
from 100m sprints to the marathon.
Blind and visually-impaired athletes
also race over a wide range of
distances, usually with a sighted
guide-runner alongside them.

Amazing performances

Paralympians are amazing athletes
and competition to win a Paralympic
gold can be fierce. This makes
UK Paralympian Dame Tanni
Grey Thompson's 11 Paralympic
golds as a wheelchair athlete
all the more impressive.

Paralympians are divided into different
classes. Their class number will start with a T if
they take part in a track event and an F if it is a
field event.

11–13: Blind and visually-impaired athletes
32–38: Athletes with cerebral palsy
40: Includes people who suffer from dwarfism
42–46: Amputees
51–58: Athletes with a spinal cord disability

Some records include:
- 100m T44 class – 10.91 seconds, Oscar Pistorius
  (South Africa), 2008 Beijing
- 800m T13 class – 1 minute, 54.78 seconds,
  Abdelilah Mame (Morocco), 2008 Beijing
- 800m T54 class – 1 minute, 45.19 seconds,
  Chantal Petitclerc (Canada), 2008 Beijing
- 200m T54 class – 27.52 seconds, Chantal
  Petitclerc (Canada), 2008 Beijing
- 100m T12 – 10.75 seconds, Adekundo Adesoji
  (Nigeria), 2004 Athens

Timeline and winner tables

1896 The first modern Olympics is held in Athens, Greece.

1912 The IAAF is formed to run world athletics.

1928 The first Olympics at which women are allowed to compete in athletics in just five events (100m, 800m, high jump, discus and 4x100m).

1934 The first European Athletics Championships is held in Turin, Italy.

1948 Fanny Blankers-Koen of the Netherlands becomes the first female athlete to win four gold medals in a single Olympics.

1951 The first Asian Games and first Pan American Games are held.

1952 The first international event for athletes with a disability is held at Stoke Mandeville Hospital in England.

1960 The first Paralympic Games is held at the same venues as the Olympics, in Rome.

1968 American Bob Beamon smashes the world long jump record by 55cm. His 8.90m record stands for 23 years.

1976 The first use of specialised racing wheelchairs in track events at the Montreal Paralympics, Canada.

1984 The women's pentathlon is replaced by heptathlon at the Olympics and in athletics in general.

1985 The first World Indoor Championships is held in Paris, France.

1988 The Seoul Paralympics is the first to feature more than 3,000 athletes with a disability.

1996 The women's 5,000m is added to the Olympics.

1998 The IAAF Golden League series of meetings begins.

2000 The Sydney Olympics adds the women's hammer throw and women's pole vault to its athletics events.

2007 The Pan American Games in Rio de Janeiro, Brazil.

2008 The Beijing Olympics sees the 3,000m women's steeplechase debut and three gold medals for Usain Bolt.

2010 The European Championships in Barcelona, Spain.

2011 The Pan American Games in Guadalajara, Mexico.

2012 The European Championships in Helsinki, Finland.

2012 The London Olympics.

2015 The Pan American Games in Toronto, Canada.

2016 The Rio de Janeiro Olympics.

Don Quarrie (right) won gold medals at both the Olympics and Pan American Games during his career.

World records

The following world records are held in some of the most common track and field events. The athlete's nationality is shown in brackets.

Men's World Records - Track

100m 9.58 Usain Bolt (Jamaica) Berlin, 2009	**200m** 19.19 Usain Bolt (Jamaica) Berlin, 2009	**400m** 43.18 Michael Johnson (USA) Seville, 1999	**800m** 1:41.11 Wilson Kipketer (Denmark) Cologne, 1997
1,500m 3:26.00 Hicham El Guerrouj (Morocco) Rome, 1998	**5,000m** 12:37.35 Kenenisa Bekele (Ethiopia) Hengelo, the Netherlands, 2004	**10,000m** 26:17.53 Kenenisa Bekele (Ethiopia) Brussels, 2005	**Marathon** 2 hours 3:59 Haile Gebreselassie (Ethiopia) Berlin, 2008
110m hurdles 12.87 Dayron Robles (Cuba) Ostrava, Czech Republic, 2008	**400m hurdles** 46.78 Kevin Young (USA) Barcelona, 1992	**4x100m relay** 37.10 Jamaica team Beijing, 2008	**4x400m relay** 2:54.29 USA team Stuttgart, 1993

Men's World Records - Field

High jump 2.45m Javier Sotomayor (Cuba) Salamanca, Spain, 1993	**Long jump** 8.95m Mike Powell (USA) Tokyo, 1991
Pole vault 6.14m Sergey Bubka (Ukraine) Sestriere, Italy, 1994	**Triple jump** 18.29m Jonathan Edwards (UK) Gothenburg, Sweden, 1995
Shot put 23.12m Randy Barnes (USA) Westwood, California, USA, 1990	**Discus** 74.08m Jürgen Schult (East Germany) Neubrandenburg, 1986
Hammer 86.74m Yuriy Sedykh (Soviet Union) Stuttgart, 1986	**Javelin** 98.48m Jan Železný (Czech Republic) Jena, Germany, 1996

Women's World Records - Track

100m 10.49 Florence Griffith Joyner (USA) Indianapolis, 1988	**200m** 21.34 Florence Griffith Joyner (USA) Seoul, 1988	**400m** 47.60 Marita Koch (East Germany) Canberra, Australia, 1985	**800m** 1:53.28 Jarmila Kratochvilová (Czechoslovakia) Munich, Germany, 1983
1,500m 3:50.46 Qu Yunxia (China) Beijing, 1993	**5,000m** 14:11.15 Tirunesh Dibaba (Ethiopia) Oslo, Norway, 2008	**10,000m** 29:31.78 Wang Junxia (China) Beijing, 1993	**Marathon** 2 hours 15:25 Paula Radcliffe (UK) London, 2003
100m hurdles 12.21 Yordanka Donkova (Bulgaria) Stara Zagora, Bulgaria, 1988	**400m hurdles** 52.34 Yuliya Pechonkina (Russia) Tula, Russia, 2003	**4x100m relay** 41.37 East Germany team Canberra, Australia, 1985	**4x400m relay** 3:15.17 Soviet Union team Seoul, 1988

Women's World Records - Field

High jump 2.09m Stefka Kostadinova (Bulgaria) Rome, Italy, 1987	**Long jump** 7.52m Galina Chistyakova (Soviet Union) St. Petersburg, 1988
Pole vault 5.06m Yelena Isinbayeva (Russia) Zurich, Switzerland, 2009	**Triple jump** 15.50m Inessa Kravets (Ukraine) Gothenburg, Sweden, 1995
Shot put 22.63m Natalya Lisovskaya (Soviet Union) Moscow, 1987	**Discus** 76.80m Gabriele Reinsch (East Germany) Neubrandenburg, Germany, 1988
Hammer 77.96m Anita Wlodarczyk (Poland) Berlin, 2009	**Javelin** 72.28m Barbora Špotáková (Czech Republic) Stuttgart, 2008

Glossary and further info

Amateur To take part for fun or the challenge of competing without being paid.

Amputee A person who has lost most or all of an arm or leg.

Appearance fee Money paid to an athlete for taking part in a particular athletics meeting or competition.

Baton The short hollow cylinder, passed between relay runners in a race.

Decade A period of ten years such as the eighties (1980–89) or the nineties.

Decathlon A men's combined event made up of ten individual track-and-field events where athletes score points for their performances in each event.

Discipline A particular athletics event, such as the 100m or long jump.

Elite The top level of athletes who are professional and paid to compete in athletics meetings.

Field events Events where athletes compete against each other trying to throw, vault or jump the highest or furthest.

Grand prix In athletics, grand prix means a type of major athletics meeting featuring professional athletes.

Heptathlon The seven discipline event for female athletes.

Host The country or city that holds an athletics event.

IAAF Short for the International Association of Athletics Federations, the organisation that runs world athletics.

Impairment A condition that can prevent a part of the body, such as the eyes, from working properly.

Marathon An athletics race run over 42.195 kilometres (26.2 miles).

Olympic village The facilities which house more than 10,000 athletes competing at an Olympic Games.

Paralympics An international competition for elite athletes with a disability.

Personal best An athlete's best ever time, distance or height for an athletics event.

Professional To be paid to compete in athletics events.

Race walkers Athletes who take part in a long-distance walking event where one foot must be in contact with the ground at all times.

Relay Races for four runners per team who each run the same distance around the track and pass on a hollow tube called a baton.

Soviet Union A country in Europe and North Asia from 1922 to 1991, made up of Russia, the Ukraine and over a dozen other republics.

Stadia The plural of stadium, the sporting arena inside which major athletics events are held.

Track events Events where athletes compete against each other in running or walking races.

World record The best ever performance in a particular athletics event, such as the women's discus or the men's 1,500m. The record must be agreed by the IAAF.

Websites

http://www.iaaf.org
The International Association of Athletics Federations' official website is full of facts, news and a calendar of forthcoming athletics events.

http://www.olympic.org/uk/index_uk.asp
The official website of the International Olympic Committee (IOC) which runs the Olympic Games. The website is packed with features, stories and results from past games.

http://london2012.com
The official website of the 2012 Olympics and Paralympics, hosted in London.

http://www.european-athletics.org
A website all about the European Championships and other competitions and events in Europe.

http://www.gbrathletics.com/ic
This website is packed with details and statistics about results from world championships and other leading athletics events.

http://www.uka.org.uk
The home page for United Kingdom Athletics, the organisation that runs athletics in the UK.

http://www.usatf.org
Biographies and news about the USA's national track and field team can be found at this website.

http://www.paralympic.org
The official website of the International Paralympic Committee contains profiles of famous paralympic athletes and details of future competitions.

http://www.nycmarathon.org
The official website of the New York City Marathon with lots of details and videos of previous marathons.

http://www.virginlondonmarathon.com
The official website of the London Marathon includes details and photos of the course, past participants and details of how runners can apply to take part.

http://www.athletix.org
A news and records website for athletics with all the latest details of winning performances by athletes.

http://www.guadalajara2011.org.mx/eng/index.asp
Information on sports, events and news of qualifying can be found at the official website for the 2011 Pan American Games in Mexico.

http://www.sporting-heroes.net/athletics-heroes/default.asp
A large collection of biographies, some long, some short, of leading athletes of the past. The collection is searchable by athlete's name, country or event.

Further reading

Training To Succeed: Athletics – Rita Storey (Franklin Watts, 2009)
This book follows a number of young athletes as they train and compete.

Sporting Skills: Athletics – Clive Gifford (Wayland, 2008)
A step-by-step guide to the techniques used in performing different athletics events.

Athletics Know The Game – UK Athletics (A&C Black, 2006)
A detailed look at the rules and skills required in track and field athletics.

Index